Disney

This magical book belongs to:

_____

ALICE
in
WONDERLAND

One summer's day, Alice and her kitten, Dinah, were listening as Alice's sister read aloud from a history book.

But Alice was getting very sleepy. She was dreaming of a world where cats and rabbits wore clothes and lived in little houses. She picked up Dinah and climbed down from the tree.

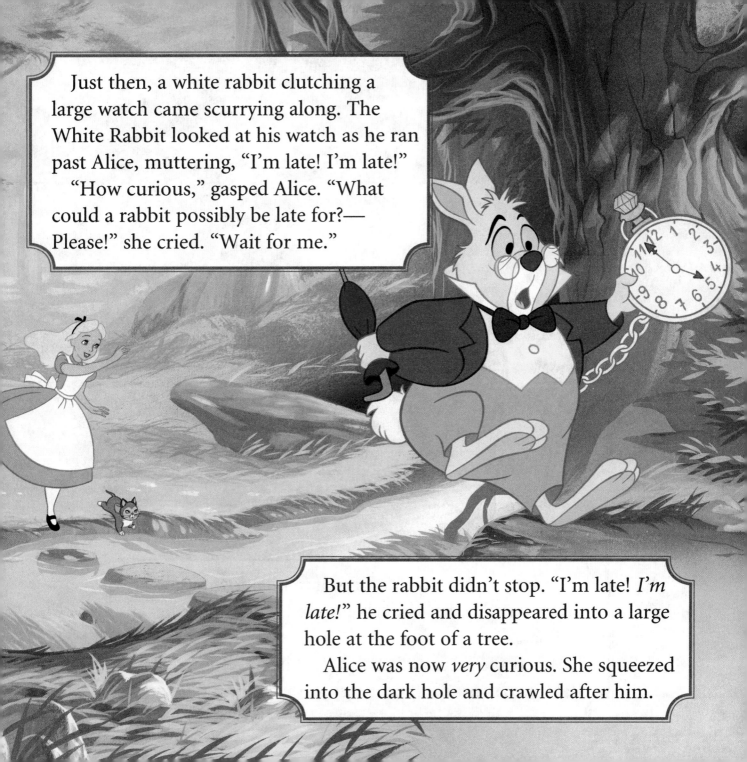

Just then, a white rabbit clutching a large watch came scurrying along. The White Rabbit looked at his watch as he ran past Alice, muttering, "I'm late! I'm late!"

"How curious," gasped Alice. "What could a rabbit possibly be late for?— Please!" she cried. "Wait for me."

But the rabbit didn't stop. "I'm late! *I'm late!*" he cried and disappeared into a large hole at the foot of a tree.

Alice was now *very* curious. She squeezed into the dark hole and crawled after him.

    Suddenly, Alice found herself falling down, down,
down. Luckily, her dress ballooned out and she began
to float.

    When she landed gently at the bottom, the White
Rabbit was just disappearing through a tiny door.

Alice tried the Doorknob.

"Eek!" cried a voice—the Doorknob was speaking!

"I'm looking for the White Rabbit," said Alice. "Please let me through."

"Sorry! You're *much* too big," replied the Doorknob. "Try the bottle on the table over there."

Alice saw the bottle labeled DRINK ME, and tasted a little. Soon, she had finished *every* drop.

Then she began to shrink! Alice became so tiny that she was able to get through the little door.

On the other side of the door, Alice found herself in the strangest place. There were talking birds and walking fish, bread-and-butterflies, and other most unusual insects.

Then Alice saw the White Rabbit through the trees in the distance—but her way was suddenly blocked by two fat little men—Tweedledum and Tweedledee.

"My name is Alice," she said. "I'm curious to know where the White Rabbit is going."

The two little men both began talking at the same time. Alice couldn't understand what they were saying, so she simply set off in another direction.

Walking along, Alice heard singing. She turned to see a toothy smile and a pair of eyes.

As Alice looked more closely, an odd-looking cat with purple stripes appeared.

"I'm Alice—and I'm looking for the White Rabbit," she said. "Which way should I go?"

"I'm the Cheshire Cat," said the odd-looking cat. "And if *I* was looking for a White Rabbit, I'd ask the Mad Hatter or the March Hare. *That* way." And he pointed toward a path in the forest.

So Alice followed the path and soon heard the Mad Hatter and the March Hare singing. They were having tea at a big table set with many places.

"We're having an un-birthday party," said the Mad Hatter. "We have only one birthday a year, so there are three hundred and sixty-four un-birthdays!"

Alice laughed out loud. "Why, then, today is my un-birthday, too!" she announced happily.

"It is?" the Mad Hatter said. "What a small world!" Tipping his hat in honor of Alice, he removed from under it a lovely un-birthday cake, which he presented to her with a flourish.

Then the Mad Hatter and the March Hare joined hands and danced around her, singing a very merry un-birthday song.

Suddenly a Dormouse jumped out of a teapot and ran around the table!

"Catch him!" called the Mad Hatter.

"No time! No time! I'm late!" cried the White Rabbit, magically appearing—and then magically disappearing into the distance.

"Wait!" shouted Alice.

By now, Alice was tired of the strange ways of Wonderland. "I'm going home," she said, just as a door in a nearby tree opened.

Stepping through it, Alice found herself in the palace gardens. She was amazed to see two playing cards painting white roses with red paint!

And there was the White Rabbit announcing—the Queen of Hearts! The Queen walked right up to Alice and said:

"Do you play croquet?"

"Yes, Your Majesty," Alice said.

"Then let the game begin," ordered the Queen.

Alice had never seen such a curious croquet game before. The balls were hedgehogs and the mallets were flamingos!

As the Queen was about to take a shot with her flamingo, the Cheshire Cat appeared. The Queen's flamingo panicked. In the confusion, the Queen lost her balance and fell over.

She was furious. "Off with her head!" she yelled at Alice.

"Shouldn't I have a trial first?" Alice said.

And so Alice was put on trial!

The first witness was the March Hare. Then came the Dormouse, followed by the Mad Hatter.

And then the Cheshire Cat appeared.

"Look, Your Majesty," said Alice. "The Cheshire Cat."

Immediately, the Dormouse jumped out of his teapot. He ran up and down the courtroom squeaking. Everyone chased after him!

The Queen began yelling at Alice
again. "Off with her—"
But before the Queen could finish,
Alice said, "You don't frighten me.
You're just a bad-tempered old Queen!"
Then Alice fled the courtroom.

Alice ran and ran, and was soon lost in a maze of hedges. She could still hear the Queen's voice but it sounded very far away now—as if in a dream. Wonderland faded, and she could hear someone calling her....

"Alice, please wake up! You've been asleep for a *very* long time." It was her sister.

Alice rubbed her eyes, and woke up on the riverbank.

"You've been dreaming," her sister said.

"Oh! I've had such an exciting time," Alice replied. "There was a White Rabbit and I followed him and…"

"Never mind," said Alice's sister. "It's time to go home for tea."

Alice picked up her kitten. "You know, Dinah," she said, "maybe I'll stay in the real world after all."